Then he saved their lives, and they swore never to leave him.

We give you the Secret-Hairy-Snot-Tooth Oath of Devotion.

When he moved house, Billy found ANOTHER monster.

Hello. My name's Sparkle-Bogey.

One thing was certain – Billy's life would never be the same **AGAIN**...

Contents

USBORNE

BILLY AND THE MINI MONSTERS

MONSTERS ON A SLEEPOVER

Illustrated by

ZANNA DAVIDSON · MELANIE WILLIAMSON

Meet Billy...

Billy was just an ordinary boy living an ordinary life, until **ONE NIGHT** he found five **MINI MONSTERS** in his sock drawer.

Gloop   Peep   Fang-Face   Captain Snott   Trumpet

Chapter 1
Packing to Go

Billy was busy packing his bag, getting ready for a **SLEEPOVER PARTY**. It was going to be his FIRST EVER SLEEPOVER.

"It's only next door, at Ash's house," Billy told his **Mini Monsters**, "but I want to make sure I've got everything. So I've made a list..."

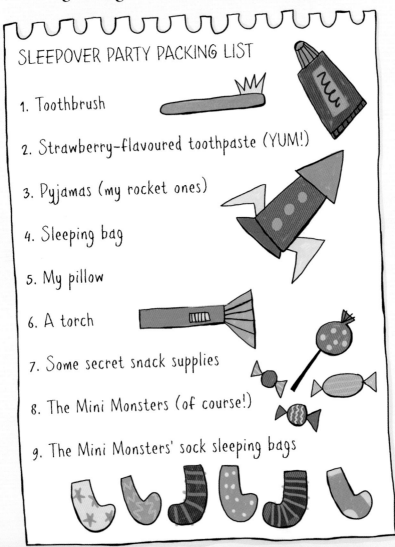

SLEEPOVER PARTY PACKING LIST

1. Toothbrush

2. Strawberry-flavoured toothpaste (YUM!)

3. Pyjamas (my rocket ones)

4. Sleeping bag

5. My pillow

6. A torch

7. Some secret snack supplies

8. The Mini Monsters (of course!)

9. The Mini Monsters' sock sleeping bags

"Who else is coming to the sleepover?" asked Trumpet.

"Jack, Sam and Ahmed," said Billy. "It's going to be AMAZING!"

Then Billy's sister, Ruby, came in. "You're so lucky," she said, watching Billy pack. "I wish *I* was going on a sleepover."

We're going to watch a movie. And stay up till MIDNIGHT!

"Mum said we could watch a film here, too," said Ruby, "so I don't feel left out. AND we're going to have hot chocolate and light the fire."

Oh.

Billy wasn't sure he liked the idea of his family being together **without him.**

It didn't feel right.

"And you're really brave going on a sleepover. I think I'd be **SCARED**," Ruby went on. "Being on a **STRANGE floor**

in a **STRANGE room**

in a **STRANGE house.**"

Billy gulped. He hadn't thought about all those things.

What if I get scared in the night?

Or I want a glass of water?

And what if I hear spooky noises?

"Ash won't be scared," thought Billy, "as it's *his* house. And Jack isn't scared of ANYTHING! Sam and Ahmed are really tough, too."

What if I'm the ONLY scared one?

"Are you okay, Billy?" asked Gloop. "You look really worried."

"Maybe going on a sleepover is a TERRIBLE idea," said Billy.

"I've never spent a **WHOLE NIGHT** in someone else's house before," Billy said, in a small voice.

You'll be fine, Billy, because you've got us!

We're coming too, remember!

All SUPER SIX of us!

"Oh yes," said Billy, taking a deep breath. "I've got my **MINI MONSTERS**. And it's Ash's house, where I've been **lots** of times before."

That's when Billy realized he could feel *two* very different things at the same time. "Now I'm nervous **AND** excited," he said.

Just then, Billy's mum called up the stairs. "Are you ready to go, Billy?"

"Nearly!" said Billy. "I'm just going to finish my packing."

Once Ruby had left, Billy zipped up his bag and turned to the Mini Monsters.

"Are you ready to go?" he asked.
"We're packed and ready," said
Captain Snott. "Let's make this

the **BEST**
SLEEPOVER EVER!"

Let's make sure we've got everything we need.

I've packed a bottle of glitter!

And some extra treats, in case we get hungry in the night.

I'm bringing my nightcap and eye mask.

And I'm taking my new glittery cape that Sparkle-Bogey made for me.

18

Chapter 2
Sweet and Sour

By the time Billy arrived at Ash's house, everyone else was there too.

"Hi Billy! Come on in," said Ash's mum, Michelle.

Billy gave his mum a quick, tight hug and stepped inside.

"Billy!" said Ash's dad, Dele. "I hope you're hungry, because we've cooked A LOT of food for you boys!"

"Naomi and I helped Dad cook!" said Ash, proudly. "Let me tell you what we're having..."

We've got coconut-fried plantain...

jollof rice...

spicy meat stew...

breadfruit...

abacha salad...

and okro soup.

"Wow!" said Jack.

"And best of all," said Ash, "we've got **puff-puff** for pudding!"

"What's that?" asked Billy.

Delicious dumplings covered in sugar!

As they took their seats, Billy popped the **Mini Monsters** under his chair. All through the meal, he kept passing them little pieces of food, so they could enjoy it too.

I love plantain.

So do I!

Ash looked down and grinned. He knew about the **Mini Monsters** now, and still got really excited every time he saw them.

"And now," said Ash, when everyone had finished, "it's

MOVIE TIME!"

Ash's mum put on a superhero film and his dad handed round popcorn.

After the movie, they raced upstairs to Ash's bedroom. All their sleeping bags were laid out in a row on the floor.

Everyone put on their pyjamas.

Look! Ours are matching!

"What shall we do first?" asked Ash.

"I've got some **amazing** sweets," said Sam. "They're sweet and sour at the same time. Who wants to try them?"

Me!

Me!

Me!

Billy put one in his mouth.

Ooh.
It's actually
really tasty.

Oh no. Now
my mouth feels
like it's about to
explode!

It's like eating a
**DEADLY
LEMON**.

"Sam, I dare you to eat THREE AT ONCE," said Jack.

"Four!" said Ash.

"You're on!" said Sam.

He put four in his mouth and kept chewing, even though his face went **really** red.

I did it!

"Do you want to try my jelly beans? They're even MORE disgusting!" said Jack.

"*Not really*," thought Billy, but he kept quiet.

"Some are **YUMMY** and others are incredibly **REVOLTING** like rotten egg," said Jack. "But the best part is – you don't know which one you're going to get!"

When all the jelly beans had gone, Ash put on some music and they danced around the room.

"*This is so great,*" thought Billy. "*Why was I ever worried about this sleepover? I'm having so much fun!*"

Then, all of a sudden, Sam went green and put his hand over his mouth. "Oh no," he said. "I think I'm going to be...

SICK!"

32

34

35

Chapter 3
Lights Off!

Everyone watched Sam turn **greener** and **greener**.

"I want my mum!" he cried.

Uh oh!

"Help!" Ash called out the door. Ash's dad came running up the stairs, took one look at Sam and hurried him to the bathroom.

The others waited, hoping Sam was okay.

FLUSH!

"Poor Sam," said Ash. "I feel terrible. It's a really **bad** sleepover, isn't it?"

"No, it's not," said Billy, trying to comfort him. "We can still have loads of fun."

And I'm sure Sam will feel better soon.

Then Ash's mum popped her head round the door.

"We're going to keep an eye on Sam downstairs for a bit," she said, "to make sure he's okay."

"Time to brush your teeth and go to sleep."

And no more sweets!

After Ash's mum had gone, Ahmed flicked on his torch.

So, who wants to hear a **SCARY STORY?**

Me! I love scary stories.

"Make it your **SCARIEST story ever!**" said Jack.

"Oh no," thought Billy. He hated scary stories. But he didn't want to say anything out loud.

Ahmed started telling his tale...

Billy burrowed into his sleeping bag, trying not to hear. But he kept catching part of the story – words like...

WITCHES

VAMPIRES

WEREWOLVES

And his **IMAGINATION** was starting to make up its own story, which was probably even **SCARIER** than Ahmed's.

Then, all of a sudden, Ahmed put his torch under his face and let out a BLOODCURDLING SCREAM!

Jack LEAPED out of his sleeping bag. "I don't like this!" he cried.

I want to go
HOME!

Then he *ran* out
of the room.

"Oh no," said Ash.
"It's even worse than
a *bad* sleepover. It's a
REALLY TERRIBLE SLEEPOVER.

We started off with five of us...
and now there are only
THREE LEFT!"

44

45

46

47

Chapter 4
Caterpillars

After Jack left, Ahmed, Billy and Ash all looked at each other.

"I'm really sorry for scaring Jack," said Ahmed.

I thought he was enjoying it.

"Don't worry," said Ash. "I'll go and check on him."

When Ash came back, he looked even more upset than before.

Ash was looking so sad, Billy
wanted to find a way to cheer
him up.

"Let's play at being caterpillars
in our sleeping bags!" said Billy.

"Ruby and I play and it's really fun."

So they got into their sleeping bags and rolled around on top of each other, laughing **a lot**.

Then Billy decided it would be really fun to do a **caterpillar dive...**

But he knocked the bedside table. Ash's light started...

...wibbling

...and **wobbling.**

Then it **toppled** over...

...and landed

SMASH

on Ahmed's foot...

...and a little bit of the lamp broke off and rolled across the carpet.

Ahmed screamed **very** loudly.

Owwww!

Then the door opened. "What's happened *now*?" asked Ash's dad.

Billy explained about being caterpillars and the light smashing, and Ahmed's injured foot.

Ash's dad let out a large sigh. "Don't worry," he said. "Accidents happen."

Come with me, Ahmed, and I'll look at your foot.

Ahmed hopped away. Then Ash's mum came in and took away the broken light.

After that, it was just Billy and Ash. "I'm **really** sorry," said Billy.

But it wasn't okay.

Billy knew how much Ash **LOVED** that night light and Ahmed was **INJURED** and this sleepover was a **DISASTER**.

How could he make things better?

55

58

59

Chapter 5
Storytime

The Mini Monsters came out from their cosy corner and looked up at Ash and Billy.

We want to make things better.

Only we're not sure how.

"What we want to say," said Captain Snott, "is that we know how you feel."

You do?

Yes! Sleepovers can be SO tricky.

Fang-Face clutched his teddy. "I've been feeling really scared. Just like Jack."

"And I've been feeling sick," said Sparkle-Bogey, "just like Sam."

"And Ahmed and I have both been INJURED!" added Gloop.

"You're right," said Ash. "Sleepovers *are* tricky. Maybe it was all a really bad idea."

"It wasn't a bad idea," said Captain Snott. "You got all your friends together and that's a **great thing!** And I had a thought..."

I'll be your night light tonight!

Because I can **GLOW** in the dark!

"Thank you," said Ash. "That makes me feel **much** better. **Mini Monsters** are the best! Uh oh!" he added. "Footsteps! You'd better **HIDE**..."

The door was flung open and in came Jack, Sam and Ahmed.
"Hooray!" said Ash. "You're back!"

I don't feel sick anymore!

And I'm not so scared.

My foot is okay, too! I've got a big plaster.

They climbed into their sleeping bags and everyone lay there, in the darkness.

Billy could tell no one was asleep. "Shall *I* tell a story?"

"I'm not sure that's a good idea," said Jack.

"This one isn't scary, I promise!" said Billy. "It's a **great** story."

Once, there was a boy who found SIX tiny monsters in his sock drawer...

Billy told the story of his **Mini Monsters**, weaving together all their adventures.

Ooohh!

He heard the others **laugh** and **gasp** and say,

Aah!

"TELL US MORE!"

"Wow!" said Jack, when Billy came to the end. "That was the **best** story ever. Thanks, Billy."

"And you know what," said Ash, and Billy could tell he was grinning, "I know a story that's going to be just as good...

...when we tell everyone at school about our **sleepover!**"

66

"It's been the most action-packed sleepover EVER," said Ahmed. "Hooray for the FAB FIVE!"

We made it!

Goodnight FAB FIVE!

And Billy realized he felt really happy, even though he wasn't in his bed, in his own house... because he was surrounded by all his friends.

70

71

Chapter 6
Breakfast Surprise!

The next morning, everyone came downstairs to find the most **AMAZING** breakfast on the table.

"Even the napkins are in really cool shapes!" said Ahmed.

Thanks Mum and Dad.

It wasn't us. It must have been Naomi.

"It wasn't me either," said Naomi, shaking her head. "Maybe it was the fairies!"

"Well, whoever did it, *thank you!* It looks delicious," said Ash's mum.

Soon after breakfast, Billy's dad came to pick him up.

How was it?

"We ate yummy food!" said Jack.

"And we **danced**," added Ahmed.

"Then we were caterpillars," said Ash.

"And even though things went a bit wrong," said Billy, "it didn't matter, because we came through it together."

"I'll take a group photo. Smile, everyone!" said Ash's dad, holding up his camera.

When Billy got home, he ran straight up to his bedroom. Then he stuck the photo of the FAB FIVE on his bedroom wall.

FAB FIVE

"Thank you for the breakfast surprise," he said to the Mini Monsters.

"And look at all my friends," he added, gazing at the photo.

"Just like us!" said the Mini Monsters. And they put their arms around each other too.

Mini Monsters Forever!

"Hooray for the Fab Five **and** the Super Six!" said Billy. "I can't wait for our next sleepover..."

All about the MINI MONSTERS

CAPTAIN SNOTT →

LIKES EATING: bogeys.

SPECIAL SKILL:
can glow in the dark.

SCARE
FACTOR:
5/10

← GLOOP

LIKES EATING: cake.

SPECIAL SKILL:
very stre-e-e-e-tchy.
Gloop can also swallow his own
eyeballs and make them reappear
on any part of his body.

SCARE
FACTOR:
4/10

FANG-FACE →

LIKES EATING:
socks, school ties, paper, or
anything that comes his way.

SPECIAL SKILL:
has massive fangs.

SCARE
FACTOR:
9/10